I0729359

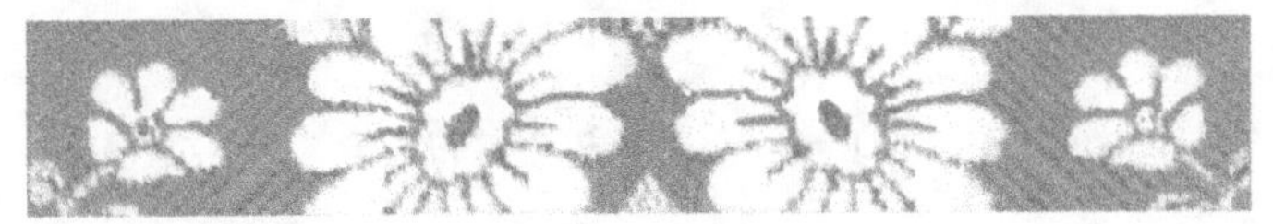

LOVE'S ARROWS
L-poems & Stories

PHYLLIS B. PARUN

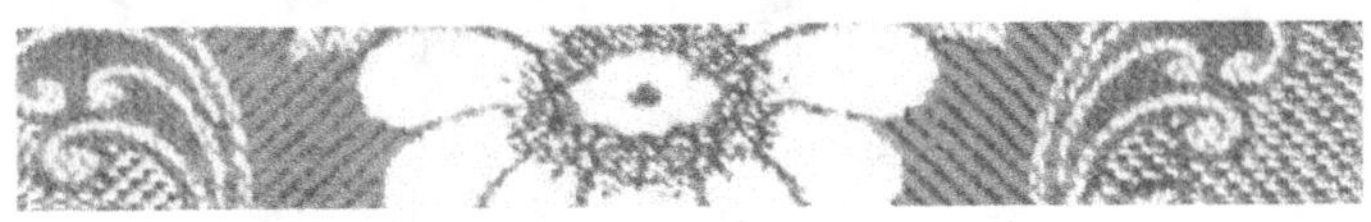

Cover Design and Illustrations by author

ISBN: 978-1-7323560-8-5

Publisher
BERNARD PRESS

Inaugural Edition

DEDICATION

To everyone who has ever loved.

CONTENTS

I

Poems

A POET'S LIFE

I keep poets hours

    writing 'til dawn

    sleeping 'til noon

    following my muse

everywhere she goes

    with the tip of my pen.

Turning the ringer off my phone

    I bask in the solitude of my home

    curl up in bed

on cold winter nights.

Pulling the covers over my head

and with my night light ballpoint

and poetry journal in hand,

I scribble down sweet phrases of

love and longing

pleasuring myself with beautiful verse

stroking the flesh of erotic words

and stoking the fires of poesy--

These are the true joys of the poet's life.

*

THAT'S A NICE TOMB

That's a nice tomb!
New Orleans is full of tombs
whole cities for the dead
above ground tombs big as houses
embellished with finely carved
figurative sculpture.

Here the Dead are dead
the living are dead -
walking dead
Everyone here is dead.

Bodies haunting the streets
taking up space
roaming around
looking for meaning
looking for love
looking for sex and drugs
Finding only the walking dead.

Tombs
City of tombs
City of living dead
walking dead
buried dead
reincarnated dead
and I, foolishly looking for a solution
to my heartbreaking sorrow
among these ruins.

*

I sit in my studio
and contemplate the nights of passion
you and I had .
memories of those kisses still linger here
where I write sweet phrases of our pleasure -
        visions of our joyful embraces
        still fill me,
I have no need for
the company of others.

I remember how you came to me
        in the heat of summer passion - and now
I am filled up with longing
        waiting for your return
        writing love verses to you.

*

Each time we make love
we were not alone.
Our naked bodies caressed,
of course,
but also
our naked hearts,
our naked souls
and our naked spirits
caressed each other.

*

Sunday morning

I found myself
hung over
and in a poetic daze,
scribbling down phrases,
composing thoughts
possessed by my muse --
For it was last night
that I got drunk on salt, sushi and tea -
though I would rather have been drunk
on your sweet lips.
But alas!
They were not available to me!

*

FOR A CHILDHOOD SWEETHEART

I cross time and space once again
just because -
when my mind drifts back
the you I knew is there
that graceful, talented, witty you
singing Verdi, Rossini, Donizetti.
What ecstasy! What beauty!
inspiration and friendship
traces still held in my heart.

*

COLLATERAL DAMAGE:
Goodbye Don't Ask Don't Tell

Growing up in
the dark ages of the 1950s when
you were my first love and I was yours
your life came crashing down around me
when your parents and mine
wanted you married to a man
and modern psychiatry used
death drugs, shock therapy, lobotomies, and
homophobic propaganda to
change us into heterosexuals
because loving our own sex
was a disease
back then.
   Goodbye Don't Ask Don't Tell

In spite of assaults
we loved right through the darkness
the marriages
the birth of children
the homophobia
the liberation wars
fighting for freedom
our freedom
to love each other
through all the years of oppression and
patronization
the story of our love told
in "The Children's Story"
and "Therese and Isabelle"
right up to "The Kids are Alright".
  Goodbye Don't Ask Don't Tell

We can never forget
the days when we could not
kiss or hold hands in public
take our lover home for family holidays
being in the closet at work and overly cautious
when looking for apartments to live in -
together;
We can never forget the anguish of denial
the looking the other way when anti-gay jokes
were told in front of us.
  Goodbye Don't Ask Don't Tell

After so many years of alienation
are we now free to write our own futures
free to live our own truths
free from our fears
even with our wounds not yet healed
and we still carry around these scars
as badges honoring the choices
we made long ago in the darkness
when we were young and it was our fate
to drive deep into the patriarchy
without each other
Are we free yet
Have we now finally driven through the darkness
and out on the other side?
  Goodbye Don't Ask Don't Tell

*

MEPHISTO

Love of you
Has reduced me to
nothing.
Every part of me
Save the Divine
Has been taken from me.

Upon your leaving
I have been stripped of myself,
my sword, my shield, my armor.
all vanishing
before me
Here I stand now
naked
for all the world to see,
vulnerable to
every danger

unprotected from
life's harm
unnourished by
your sweet intimacies

Only a small part
of my soul
remaining
And how easily I would
give up that part of me
to the love of you
for your return.

*

THE ARTIST AND HER MUSE

She looked at me.
I was drawing
focusing somewhere passed her,
passed the form that she was -
focused into another world,
a mere shadow of this one.

She looked at me
   dead at me.
She didn't look passed me,
she looked directly into my eyes.
She looked into the form
   that I was,
breaking my poetic trance
severing it into pieces -
My trance shattered
fell down around me.

*S*he was my model

I was her

muse.

*

PILGRIMAGE TO PARIS
and The Père Lachaise Cemetery

Paths and paths and paths
of graves
housing artists and writers
Now dead.

Paths and paths
leading to more paths
to eternal houses of
once vibrant artists.
It's the year 2000
and all these artists   now icy cold
lay in this damp, stony place.

Paris now a City of Phantoms

and still the tourists come

like so many hungry refugees

from contemporary civilization

seeking guidance from these graves

and inspiration from the streets of Paris

where these artists once walked

And from the stones they once walked upon.

*

YOU HAVE TURNED ME INTO A POET

Because of you
I have many memories of
life's sweetest pleasures
And now since your divorce of me
my sorrow casts its shadow and
my tears fertilize this poet's soil.
I am pregnant with pungent verse
poetry flowing through my veins day and night

When my body and soul call out for you
words come streaming in
I am wet with passionate phrases
Without you I keep the company of love verse
Hear the tantric passion in the words of poets
warming my heart made cold by your departure
putting fire back into the caldron of my life
While my cat keeps my hours
sleeping at my feet like a sphinx
guarding some ancestral spirit
within this temple   and comforting me.

*

Your sweet smile
leaves me yearning
to touch your lips
with mine

*

SAPPHOISMS

1

Before I met you
I was starving
And you came to feed me

2

A day without
your touch is like
being thirsty
And not having water

3

When I think of you
I think of laughter

4

I miss you
In the quiet corners of my day

5

Sweet memories of us
Are the reason
my heart still beats

6

There is no breeze
no blade of grass
that has not whispered
your name

7

You are the joyful dream
Which has been with me
My entire life

8

I awoke from dreams
Of kissing you

9

Everything you said to me

Was music

10

What I couldn't do

To get a glimpse of you.

11

The wind

And the sun

On my skin

And you

in my heart.

*

II

THREE SHORT STORIES

1

THE LETTER

A letter arrived. When she touched it she felt something strangely familiar. She brought the letter in and placed it on her desk where she could see it. There was a return address she did not recognize, but when she saw the city stamp it took her back to her youth.

Her husband had died five years previously and now at seventy-eight she was alone and even though she had two adult children, a son, Alan, and a daughter, Cassie, she did not feel less alone. The prospect of being alone into old age with children and grandchildren did not comfort her. She still felt lonely.

As she was still grieving five years later, her two children worried about her being isolated and melancholy. She felt the loss of her very best friend and the loss of her way of life. She longed for the soul connection she once had and for that deep listening of an intimate companion.

Mom, Alan and I are worried about you. We think you should start dating.

At my age! What would be the point? Besides how would I even meet someone?

Well, you would have a companion. We were wondering if there was someone in your past that you had a thing for, someone you lost track of?

From my past?

Yes, you know a sweetheart, a former date? Surely there must have been someone?

We really don't want to go back there.

Mom, we just want you to be happy and not feel so alone.

I think I'm doing fine just as I am.

Mom, sure you have wonderful memories and we would like to see you make even more of them.

I have a good life. I have you and Alan and the grandchildren.

Mom, you know that is not enough.

Well, maybe not but –

So tell me: wasn't there anyone, some sweetheart in your past?

Well —

Well? Who?

Maybe.

Maybe, who?

Ok, yes, there was.

Who?

It's not what you would think?

Mom, I am not thinking anything. So just tell me.

Well, it was a girl —

A girl? This sweetheart was a girl!

Yes.

There was a long silence. She did not know what her daughter would think of this. And she was not really "coming out" but she knew that between her early college days and today many social changes had taken place. There was a new liberalism so she chanced it hoping that her daughter, whom whom she never even talked with about this, would understand.

You mean you had a thing for a girl?

We were young and it was just a flirtation and didn't go anywhere. It was long before the gay and feminist liberation movements, you see.

How did you meet?

In college. We met in college. We were friends for several years then I met your father and we married and had you two.

But, Mom, you did feel something for her?

Yes. Yes, I did.

Mom, that is so cool.

You think so! I found it very frustrating.

No, it's cool. Really it is. So you were best friends?

More. I think it's called a "passionate friendship" isn't it?

So it was only a flirtation and never sexual?

Good heavens, no! The times were too repressive. Back then it was considered to be a disease. Our parents could have put us in a mental hospital. Besides we were supposed to get married and have kids.

Mom - how awful! Was it really like that?

Yes, it was. So we were just very close friends.

Do you think she felt the same toward you?

I am sure she did. And I suppose that if there had been more freedom then like there is now, we would have become lovers. But there wasn't and we didn't.

Aren't you glad things have changed for the better?

Yes, I suppose but that's past now.

Maybe so Mom, but then again maybe not.

Cassie did not forget this conversation and over the next several months she continued to pry information out of her mother about this young woman until she got the girl's name, where she lived and some other pertinent information. After an Internet search, Cassie found a phone number and address and then she called. From the conversation Cassie learned that the other woman had come out, that her lover of forty years had died and now she was alone also, like her Mom was. After telling her her own mother's story, Cassie suggested that the woman write and then give her mother a call.

She never did open the letter that had arrived that day, but just stared at it there on her desk for months. It blended in with all the other memories and antiques that furnished her house.

One day the phone rang

Hello!
Who is this?
You don't know?
No.
It's a voice from your past.
Who is this?
Virginia.
Virginia? Virginia!
Yes.
Virginia? Virginia! Ah -

There was a silence. Cassie thought the phone went dead.

I'm calling because your daughter called me.
She did?
Yes and then I wrote to you. Did you get my letter?
Yes. But I didn't open it.
You didn't?
No, I felt uncomfortable. You know I always felt that *you can't go home again?*
Oh, yes, I remember now. I fear you have read too much Thomas Wolfe.

Both of them just burst out laughing.

I haven't seen you in so many years. And I would like to so how about we get together?
It has been many years. And so much has changed. But why now?
It is a long story. How about we talk about it over lunch. We'll catch up.
But I don't know. This is rather sudden.

Sudden? What's sudden about getting in touch
after forty years? It's just lunch. We'll get together
and have a good talk. I'd really like to hear about
how your life turned out. You can fill me in.
Well, I suppose that would be ok.
Where shall we meet?

Why don't you come over here on Thursday? My
daughter will be here too and you can meet her.
Ok, then. I am so looking forward to seeing you.

   She got directions to their house, and on the
appointed day she buys a bouquet of long
stemmed red roses. Around noon she arrives at
the address, parks the car, walks up to the front
door and rings the bell.

She waits and then rings again. Hearing noises inside she holds the roses firmly, nervously anticipating the door opening and seeing those beautiful hazel eyes of her sweetheart from long ago. Finally, the latch turns and the door opens.

Standing there before her was a young woman with long flowing dark brown hair, much too young to be her former friend. For a moment neither said anything. They were both stunned into silence by recognition of each other. They had met at the college where she was a professor and this young woman was a student. This was a summer student who had come onto her and who she had reluctantly rebuffed in order not to endanger her tenure status at the college. That was fifteen years ago. But she always remembered her because she found her very attractive but could never act on it because of her position at the college.

As they both stood there looking at each other, memories of their past flirtations flashed before them, when she heard a woman's voice from inside the house say,

"Cassie is that her? Do invite her in."

Just then she lost her firm grip and the red roses slipped from her hand, falling to the porch floor in front of her.

*

2

ENCORE

So many years
and yet it seems as if they weren't there at all
except
we are meeting now
not then.

It started as a letter
one singular letter
then two, then three,
with each I remembered more
I saw scenes
heard sounds
smelled aromas
all the way back
to the first day we met

Now once again
I am in Paris
crisscrossing that city's ancient geometry
through cosmic time and space

Time stands still in my memory
there she is the same
here I am the same
nothing changed
in the absence
in the silence
in the distance between
since the day we first fell in love
those many years ago.

Will she remember
so many years ago
when we were young and so beautiful?
Will she
I wonder.

The taxi arrives at Opéra Palais Garnier

The driver lets me out.

I step through those grand doors

into the gilded Baroque opulence of

the Second Empire

climbing its magnificent staircase

to my box *pour l'amour*

one glance

at the opera program

I knew.

The lights dimmed

the strings played that proud majestic,

funereal overture

chorus voices part the curtain

and I am transported to 1775 the Paris

of Gluck and Orfeo's first performance

of love lost once, love lost twice

and twice regained.

Then a single unforgettable voice sores above the

rest.

It is hers

as I remember her

my heart is brought to a stand still.

And when she sang

"Che faro senza Euridice? Dove andro

 senza il mio ben?"

"What can I do without Euridice? How can I live

without my love?"

I fell hopelessly under her spell a second time

as if her eyes met mine for the very first time

"Euridice! Euridice!" as if singing

a passionate plea for me, her lover, to return

the bel canto cry

"O Dio! Rispondi! Rispondi."

the memory of those times

when we were younger

and I followed her from stage to stage

from audience to audience

here I was in Paris falling in love all over again.

The three acts passed like a dream
and I sat transfixed for an eternity until the curtain
then finally, arising from my seat I left the box
making my way down the staircase backstage
flowers and a card preceding me
to her dressing room door

I knocked once
twice, three times.
It opened.
There she was
standing before me
emerging from my dream stretching back thirty years.
Without any hesitation I took her in my arms
kissing her passionately on the lips

"I've been wanting to do that ever since
our eyes first met those many years ago."
"All that matters now is we are here
together now."

She took my arm,
as we left 19thcentury opulence behind
for a stroll down the Place de l'Opéra
passing the Café de la Paix and
Belle Époque Paris
hailing a taxi headed for the early 20thcentury,
the feel of the cobble Parisian streets
beneath the wheels,
we arrived at the Saint-Germain des Paris
and the Les Deux Margot where
the driver lets us out.

Her hand in mine we chose a table

in full view of the Paris streets

and sat down to tea

in the company

of the ghosts of all those

avant-garde artists and writers

who graced these tables decades ago.

And so it began again

just as it had so many years ago.

*

3

BAILEY'S STORMS

It was the beginning of the hurricane season when last we met one afternoon over a stormy meal at Bailey's. For me it was wet, very wet weather, but not the kind of wet a woman can truly enjoy on such an afternoon.

I was in green and she in white on this rainy day as we sat in a secluded corner of her choosing getting comfortable for what I thought was going to be an entirely pleasant rendezvous. How wrong I was for that was not what was to transpire on that day.

It has been several months, which seemed like an eternity since we had not conversed at all even by voice mail. It seemed to me that she had gotten busy with work, which overshadowed even the previous passion she had displayed for our friendship.

She had always been difficult. She never was really obvious with her feelings even though she was extraordinarily passionate and romantic. But she was never capable of anything really ordinary and this is why I found her so utterly fascinating and why it was so impossible for me to consider being without her.

Now as we sat there together for the first time in months, she looking into my eyes and I into hers, I felt at peace, the kind of peace one has from being held in her arms and caressed gently by her voice.

She began by telling me that she did not think we should continue telephone tag and I was feeling that even telephone tag was better than nothing, painful though it was not to have more.

She always left me wanting more, longing for her companionship night and day. I craved the sound of her voice and now she was saying that we should let things lay "fallow" for a while. What a blow that struck in my heart. How tender, how sensitive I was at her every mood change, at her every word. This struck like a funeral; suddenly, I felt someone had died.

It's not true that I have never experienced grief because I have. I am no stranger to grief. Grief has been my constant companion since my mother's death when I was a teen. But this, this was such a shock. How easily my tears flowed, how silly I felt, how embarrassed I was to have a show of emotion in a public restaurant.

Still there was this loss, and I grieved for all the loves I'd had had and lost, and for all the joys and depths of feeling this one woman had engendered in me over the last three years. She had been my mother to hold onto and my sister to play with. She had been my colleague, my teacher, my best friend. I had learned so much from her about being intimate with a woman. She had calmed me. She had guided me. She had been my nurturer, my counselor, my teacher, and friend. We had been as close as two women could possibly have been without any sexual expression. Life did not seem as vibrant with the prospect of her missing from it.

I sat frozen, tears streaming down my face as I remembered the many wonderful dinners with her for birthdays, anniversaries, and Christmas. One visit in particular returned to me just then. It was on Yom Kippur. When I arrived home on that afternoon I found a neighbor's note telling me that flowers had been left for me. My heart leapt. Chills consumed me. My knees became weak and I had to sit down.

I picked the flowers up from the neighbor. They were beautiful. I took them home and cut them into three bouquets. At seven-thirty with a gentle knock at the door, she arrived dressed in white, with a smile, a hug and a kiss. My heart was thumping. We sat down to a candlelight dinner and gazing into each other's eyes, talked of many things,

After dinner we danced, held hands, and kissed for what I remember as the second time. Of course, it was Yom Kippur and she had come to ask forgiveness. What a romantic way to do it!

So many meetings in restaurants. Once, I remembered, she had invited me for Chinese, leaving this message.

"I don't need to eat anything when I'm with you. I am nourished by the mere presence of being with you."

She had always been very romantic and even though she acknowledged the depth of her feelings for me in so many ways, she didn't feel this warranted changing her whole life. She was married and a mother of three. So she would go no further then flirtatious phone calls and dinners at restaurants.

Once when she had grown tired of making her daily early morning calls, and I, still attached to this intimate practice of hers, told her that I missed her daily calls. She responded that she liked "to call early in the morning when I imagine you to be asleep and whisper into your ear." Her words rushed me so, that I almost fainted like a tightly clad Victorian lady being courted.

I had talked with her many times about her flirting, her affectionate poetry, and her need for romance with a woman, but she never gave it a second thought. Yet I could not go on thinking this was a completely straight woman. She had invited, nourished and cultivated our passionate friendship. I had simply returned it.

But even though I had tried pushing and probing nothing seemed to move her at all toward recognition. Even though she had once told me that when she was a child, she had seen a picture of two women kissing and thinking that the picture was beautiful showed it to her mother. After that the book disappeared and was never mentioned again.

Now, three years after our first meeting. Her suggestions that we end our encounters tormented me.

"I want you to understand that my position has not changed," she told me, "I still can't be with you the way you want me to."

This was the woman, after all, who had run panting to get my phone calls, who had given our first kiss in a park, who's romantic early morning and late night calls I had built my day around, to whom I had written so many letters.

What a shocking ending to such a romantic affair this was indeed.

I left the restaurant that day with a heavy heart and tears in my eyes, knowing that as so many times before the weather would change and the sun would shine again.

(Before the levies broke and flooded of New Orleans in 2005, Bailey's was a popular local restaurant in the famous New Orleans Fairmont Hotel.)

III
Epilogue Poetry

The Singer

She was born with that voice
Absolute pitch, musical skill extraordinaire,
Never a faulty delivery did pass her lips
Too many words made her sick
Music   was her forte:
When she sang scales
Only a nightingale could compete
With the beauty of her sound.
She was My Fair Lady,
Lilly Pons and Maria Callas
And when she left
She took the music with her.

I could never love you
the way you wanted to be loved
and you knew it
you could not love me
the way I wanted to be loved
but I didn't know it
it took all this time to
realize it

I should have said
Please stay

Won't you come back
Just for a moment at least

Sometimes we only need one word

I love you

Sometimes three

I want you beside me

familiar and

real

thoughts of you linger still
why?
maybe its the memory of you
or the thought of you
or the decade we were in
that I long for
but then maybe
its you

break my heart once
break it again
then again
still breaking it
even now
when it is all said and done
you still grow on me

what an artist your are
creating this long lasting
appreciation

Acknowledgments

Thanks to all the many named and unnamed persons who shared their lives which became fodder for these stories.

And a special thanks to the Dancing-Shark Studio of Karen E. Doby or indispensible technical support and cover formatting. And to my readers Bobbie Geary and Gloria Daniel always generous with their insightful commenets.

PHYLLIS PARUN

New Orleans born, artist-philosopher poet, was raised and educated by Louisiana teacher parents from whom she learned the art of living well through art, dance, music and sports, pursued the study of philosophy at Louisiana State University in New Orleans, the University of Pennsylvania and LSU Baton Rouge. While teaching at Dillard University, Ms. Parun received a grant to attend Harvard in the social sciences. Ms. Parun spent a large part of her adult life in the visual arts as arts-activist, initiating the city's first 1% for Arts Ordinance, operating a Fine and Decorative Arts Studio, restoring antiques and reviving the lost gilded arts. As an arts, health and political activist, Ms. Parun has been a catalyst, shaping the unwritten culture of the New Orleans landscape.

Ms. Parun's published genres include interviews, articles, essays, poems, e-zines, art, and photography in a wide variety of local and national publications: The Beachcomber (LSUNO), Alternatives, Contemporary Arts Southeast, Macrobiotics Today, NonCredo, The Rogue, Pulse (AOBTA), American Assn. of Oriental Medicine, MacroNetjournal, Healthways, Bywater Current, Gulf Coast Arts Review, ArtLit, Iris, Qi: Journal of Traditional Eastern Health and Fitness, The New Laurel Review (2001, 2015), The Maple Leaf Rag III (2006), Mending for Memory (2017) and creator of The New Orleans Living Treasurers Award and The New Orleans Avant-Garde ezine.

Ms. Parun's writing is filled with a wealth of fulfilling life experiences. Ms. Parun is undoubtedly one of New Orleans' native living treasures.

END NOTES

Thank you for reading.
And if you enjoyed this please leave a review at
Amazon USA
https://www.amazon.com/-
/e/B006HX9348

If you like this one you might also enjoy

**"New Orleans Born" and "New Orleans
Between Poetry and the Blues"**

And visit artist-author webpage
www.phyllisparun.com

For future notifications on new releases,

join author email list:

pbpstudio@yahoo.com

Notes

Notes